Lollylegs

PAMELA FREEMAN

ILLUSTRATED BY

RHIAN NEST JAMES

**WALKER
BOOKS**

To my brother, Paul.
PF
For Lara Pool.
RNJ

First published in Great Britain 2013 by Walker Books Ltd
87 Vauxhall Walk, London SE11 5HJ

2 4 6 8 10 9 7 5 3 1

Text © 2011 Pamela Freeman
Illustrations © 2011 Rhian Nest James

The right of Pamela Freeman and Rhian Nest James to be identified as author and illustrator respectively of this work has been asserted by them in accordance with the Copyright, Designs and Patents Act 1988

This book has been typeset in Bembo Educational

Printed and bound in China

British Library Cataloguing in Publication Data:
a catalogue record for this book is
available from the British Library

ISBN 978-1-4063-5332-7

www.walker.co.uk

A Lamb

Laura's dad brought the lamb home on a Friday.

"Here he is," Dad said. "What are you going to call him?"

Dad put him down on the kitchen table. The lamb stood and blinked at them. His legs wobbled.

Laura looked at the lamb for a long time.

"Lollylegs," she said.

Lollylegs wasn't really Laura's lamb. Dad had brought him home from the stockyards to give as a raffle prize for the school fete. Someone would get to take Lollylegs home.

"So don't get too attached to him," Mum said. "You know he's going to the fete next Saturday."

His wool was soft and tickly. He had
long lashes on his big brown eyes.

9

Laura looked
after him. She fed
him warm milk
from a baby bottle. He guzzled and
spilt the milk, butting Laura on the
hand and the arm as if that would
make the milk come faster.

He nuzzled her
under the chin.

Then he did a wee
on the floor.

"He should sleep
in the laundry,"
Dad said, while he
cleaned it up.

"He's too little!" Laura said.
"He'd be lonely."

Mum stroked Lollylegs's head.

"He *is* very little, Dave," she said
to Dad.

"Hmm," Dad said. "I suppose…"
Then he smiled at Mum, the special
smile he kept just for her. "But you get
to clean up any messes."

13

So Laura made Lollylegs a bed in her room out of rags and an old, old blanket which was thin with washing.

She took Lollylegs outside just before bedtime, and after he did what Mum called "his business", she waited while he explored the backyard. He nosed the camellia bushes and tugged a dandelion flower off its stem, then spat it out.

It was a big yard and the grass was usually a bit long because Jason, Laura's big brother, didn't like doing the lawn mowing and put it off for as long as he could.

"You'd like to live here, wouldn't you?" Laura said to Lollylegs.

She imagined Lollylegs living with
them and sighed.

"I wish you weren't going to the
fete," she said, hugging him
as hard as she could.

Lollylegs
snuggled his
head into
her armpit.
It tickled.

Laura started to laugh and she and
Lollylegs rolled around on the grass
until Mum called them inside.

Lollylegs's tail
waved so much it
looked like he was
spinning it round in a circle. Laura
knew that meant he was happy.

That night Lollylegs wouldn't settle into his bed. He would lie down while Laura was with him, but as soon as she got up and went to her bed, he did too. He made a little noise that was not quite a baa and not quite like crying. He sounded sad but determined.

"He's like Mary's little lamb!" Mum laughed. "I bet he'd follow you to school if we let him."

Laura's eyes grew wide. What a wonderful idea! She would love to take Lollylegs to school and show

him off for News. Her best friend, Caitlin, would love Lollylegs too. Laura imagined Lollylegs standing up on the teacher's desk while everyone took turns patting him. She was sure Lollylegs wouldn't mind.

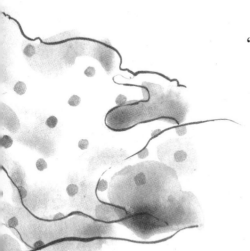

"Oh, *can* he come to
school, Mum?"
"No," Mum said,
in that tone that
meant there was
no use arguing.
"But I suppose
he can sleep
with you. It's
only for a week."
So Lollylegs curled
up on his blanket on top of
the duvet, and Laura curled up
underneath, and she went to sleep
patting Lollylegs's
soft, soft wool.

23

"Baaaa," he said very quietly.

"Baaaa," Laura said back.

"Goodnight."

Raffle Tickets

Caitlin

Jack

Daniel

Jessica

The school fete was on Saturday and all week at school the kids talked about it.

"My mum's making toffees and biscuits!" Caitlin said. "Her toffees are so good!"

"I'm going to win all the hoopla prizes," Jack boasted.

"My dad's running the bookstall," said Daniel.

"I'm going on the Ferris wheel!" Jessica said, shivering with excitement. "But my mum will come with me 'cause it's a bit scary."

27

"We're bringing a lamb to raffle," Laura said. "His name's Lollylegs."

The others looked at her for a moment.

"Cool," Jack said.

After school, Laura's big brother, Jason, poked Lollylegs in the back.

"Not much meat on him," he said. "Whoever wins will have to fatten him up a bit."

"What do you mean?" Laura asked.

"Well, four nice legs of
lamb on that," Jason said
and smacked his lips.
"Put him on a spit,
bit of salad,
you've got
a party."

"NO!" Laura shouted
and hugged Lollylegs.
He nibbled at her fingers
with soft lips.
She started to cry.
"Don't let them
kill him!"

29

Mum and Dad looked at each other
and then glared at Jason.

"Whoever wins him will probably keep him as a lawnmower," Dad said. "I know I'd like to have a sheep to eat the grass so I didn't have to wait for Jason to mow it."

"That's right," Mum said. "He'll get fat on someone's front lawn. Don't you worry about it, Laura."

But Jason smirked at Laura and she was not sure that Mum and Dad were telling the truth.

The next day at school, Laura didn't eat her morning snack.

Daniel noticed. He always ate all of his meals. If there hadn't been a school rule against sharing food, he would have eaten all of Laura's too.

"What's the matter?" Caitlin asked. "Do you feel sick?"

Laura did feel sick, but it wasn't the vomiting kind of sick. It was because every time she thought about Lollylegs being put onto a spit, her stomach got all churned up.

She told Caitlin and Jack and Jessica and Daniel what Jason had

said, and they all agreed that he was probably right.

"Your mum and dad just don't want you to be upset," Daniel said. "Parents are like that."

After that Laura didn't feel like eating her lunch either, or her snack when she got home from school.

"Are you all right, sweetheart?" Dad asked.

Laura burst into tears. "What if whoever wins Lollylegs really *does* want to … to … to *eat* him?" she sobbed. "Can't we keep him?"

34

Dad gave her a hug, but he shook his head. "I've promised the school. But we'll buy some tickets. Maybe we can win him back."

Laura sniffed away her tears. That was a good idea. She went to her piggy bank and tipped all the money out.

"How many tickets can I get for that much?" Laura asked Dad.

"Four," Dad said.

"How many tickets will they sell?"
Laura asked.

"Oh, about a hundred," Dad said.

Four tickets were not enough.
Laura had to get more money.

"How can I get money, Mum?" she asked.

"You could do jobs for people," Mum said. "You can tidy out the saucepan cupboard for me, if you like."

Laura tidied the saucepan cupboard and the tea towel drawer. That earned her enough money for another ticket.

But five tickets weren't enough.

All week, Laura did jobs for everyone.

She washed Dad's car.

She weeded
Grandma's flowerbed.

She swept up
all the leaves on
their next-door
neighbour's path.

She went through all
Mum's pegs and threw out
the broken and rusty ones.

She swept out
the garage.

She tidied her toy box and put
the toys she didn't want any more
in a box for Caitlin's little sister,
Rose.

She scrubbed the mould off the
shower cubicle, which was hard, but
kind of fun.

"That's a job I've been meaning
to do for ages," Mum said. "Thanks,
sweetheart."

"I don't know why you're bothering," Jason said. "It's just a lamb."

"It's *not* just a lamb," said Laura. "It's *Lollylegs*."

"Yeah, right," Jason said. But he paid her to clean up his room. And to shine his school shoes.

"Might as well have someone else do the work," he said.

Every morning and every night, Laura sat on the floor and held Lollylegs while she fed him his bottle.

"I won't let you be eaten!" Laura told him. He butted her middle gently, as if he understood that her stomach was full of butterflies whenever she thought about the fete and the raffle. Having Lollylegs butt her there helped, but only a bit.

The Fete

On the day of the fete, Laura put her money into one of her yellow daisy socks, for good luck. She held Lollylegs tightly in the car all the way to school.

"Don't worry," she said, "I'll look after you."

47

Mum and Dad and Laura looked
all over the fete before they found the
raffle table. Mr Benton, her teacher,
was in charge. There was a sign saying,
"Win your own lamb!"

She put Lollylegs down on the table
very carefully.

"I'd like to buy some tickets, please."

With the money she had earned and some extra that Dad had given her, Laura bought all the tickets that were left. But Mr Benton had already sold a lot of tickets to other people.

"You've bought the most tickets," he reassured Laura.

But that didn't matter. Only one ticket would be pulled out of the barrel. What if it was someone else's? Someone who wanted food for a party.

"Come and look at the fete while
we're waiting," Mum said. But Laura
shook her head.

She stood by the table
and stroked Lollylegs.

Caitlin and Jack and Jessica and
Daniel came to see him and pat him.

"He *is* very soft," Caitlin said.
Lollylegs nuzzled her fingertips gently.
"I think he likes me!"

"I bought a ticket," Jack said. "I
promise I won't eat him if I win."

"Can I come and visit him?"
Laura asked.

"Course you can," Jack said, patting
Lollylegs as if he already owned him.
"Anytime you like."

"Come on the Ferris wheel with me,
Laura," Jessica said, but Laura
shook her head.

This might be her last chance
to be with Lollylegs.

Dad came over to her.

"Don't you want to have a look round the fete, sweetheart?"

Laura shook her head. She was trying hard not to cry.

"Are you OK?"

"I feel a bit sick in the stomach," Laura said. "I wish it was over."

"Couldn't we have the draw now?"
Dad asked Mr Benton. "You've sold all
the tickets."

Mr Benton looked at Laura
and smiled.

"All right."

He made an announcement over the microphone.

"Please pay attention – the raffle for the lamb is about to take place."

A crowd gathered. Laura and Caitlin and Daniel and Jessica and Jack stood in the front row. Jack held his ticket out so he could see the number clearly. Laura held her bunch of tickets in one hand and Dad's hand in the other. She could feel the butterflies in her stomach trying to fly.

A man in the crowd said, "Nice bit of lamb on a spit, there," and Laura gripped Dad's hand tightly.

Mr Benton put his hand in the barrel
and drew out a ticket.

"And the winner is … Jason Ng."
Everyone clapped.

"Jason?" Laura
said. "But…"

Jason came over
and picked up Lollylegs.

"Oh, well, I thought, why not buy
a ticket? Seeing that you wanted him
so much."

And he put Lollylegs

into Laura's arms.